THE ADVENTURES OF MISS ANNE DE BOURGH OF ROSINGS

A PRIDE & PREJUDICE VARIATION
PREQUEL TO MR. DARCY'S BOOKSHOP

v. I

SUMMER HANFORD

Summer Hanford

Also by Summer Hanford
Mr. Darcy's Bookshop
*Mr. Darcy's Matchmaker**
*Once Upon a Time at Pemberley**

By Renata McMann & Summer Hanford
Charitable Endeavors
*Pride & Prejudice and Planets**
To Fall for Mr. Darcy
Mr. Collins' Will
More Than He Seems
After Anne
Their Secret Love
*A Duel in Meryton**
Love, Letters and Lies
*The Long Road to Longbourn**
*Hypothetically Married**
The Forgiving Season
The Widow Elizabeth
Foiled Elopement
Believing in Darcy
Her Final Wish
Miss Bingley's Christmas
Epiphany with Tea
Courting Elizabeth
The Fire at Netherfield Park
*From Ashes to Heiresses**
Entanglements of Honor
Lady Catherine Regrets
A Death at Rosings
Mary Younge
Poor Mr. Darcy
Mr. Collins' Deception
The Scandalous Stepmother
Caroline and the Footman
Elizabeth's Plight (The Wickham Coin Book II)
Georgiana's Folly (The Wickham Coin Book I)

The Second Mrs. Darcy

Joint Collections:

A Dollop of Pride and a Dash of Prejudice:
Includes from above: *Their Secret Love, Miss Bingley's Christmas, Epiphany with Tea* and *From Ashes to Heiresses*.

Pride and Prejudice Villains Revisited – Redeemed – Reimagined A Collection of Six Short Stories.
Includes: *Lady Catherine Regrets, Mary Younge, Mr. Collins' Deception* and *Caroline and the Footman,* along with two the additional flash fiction pieces, *Mrs. Bennet's Triumph* and *Wickham's Journal.*

Georgiana's Folly & Elizabeth's Plight: Wickham Coin Series, Volumes I & II
Includes from above: *Elizabeth's Plight* and *Georgiana's Folly*.

By Renata McMann
Why Wed

Heiress to Longbourn
Pemberley Weddings
The Inconsistency of Caroline Bingley
Three Daughters Married
Anne de Bourgh Manages
The above five works are collected in the book:
Five Pride and Prejudice Variations

*available as an audio book

THE ADVENTURES OF MISS ANNE DE BOURGH OF ROSINGS

CHAPTER ONE

Spring, 1797

Anne paced the lawn beneath the broad-limbed tree. At fourteen, she could climb better than any of her cousins, but it was Darcy who sat on one of the wide branches that swept out parallel to the ground about four feet up. The old oak, which had stood beside Rosings for over two hundred years, boasted many such aerial highways and was, therefore, a favorite of theirs. Below Darcy, Richard leaned against the trunk as he worked to get a blade of grass to whistle, not paying Anne much attention, but Darcy stoically watched her pace.

"I cannot believe Henry took my apple tart," Anne groused. "He knew that tart was mine, and he'd already eaten his, and he simply took it and ate it, and smirked at me while he chewed. Richard, your brother is horrid."

"Yes," Richard agreed, then put the blade of grass to his lips and blew. A high-pitched whistle shrieked forth. "He is. Always has been. That's why we don't include him."

"This cannot be allowed to go unpunished," Anne declared. "It's the principle of the matter."

"Quite right," Darcy said, swinging his legs. "He knew the tart was yours and he ate it anyhow. Moreover, he told you to stuff it when you complained. He was greedy and a bully. Two things we must stand against on principle."

"Those aren't the principles I'm talking about," Anne said, still pacing. "I'm talking about the principle that if someone steals my apple tart and then refuses to apologize, I must get revenge."

"I don't think that's how the word 'principle' works," Darcy said.

Anne cast him a glare as she stomped past, her Hessians trampling the grass under the oak. "It's one of my principles, Darcy."

"How will you get him back?" Richard asked, tossing the now damp blade of grass to the ground and scrubbing his palms on his breeches. "My father and Uncle Lewis aren't going to care about an apple tart."

"My father might care," Darcy supplied.

Both his and Richard's fathers were visiting Anne's papa, Sir Lewis, at Rosings. Since all their wives were deceased and none saw any reason to remarry, even Anne's papa who had only her, a daughter, the three gentlemen took turns hosting one another. "I don't want to tattle on him," Anne said firmly. "I want revenge. I would challenge him, but he'll refuse to accept."

"He won't accept because you're a girl," Darcy concurred from his tree branch.

"He won't accept because Anne's better than he is at fencing," Richard corrected.

"And he knows it," Anne added smugly. Nor was her smugness undeserved. As he had no son, Sir Lewis had hired the finest fencing, shooting, boxing, and riding instructors for Anne. She was everything he'd always wanted in his heir, aside from being female, but Sir Lewis had decided to ignore that the moment his beloved Catherine died without providing a son.

"You could challenge him to a race," Darcy said.

Richard shook his head. "Anne's a better rider than Henry, too."

"And besides," Anne said as she stomped back past, "I don't need to prove which of us is in the right by besting him. I know I'm in the right and he is in the wrong. I want vengeance, Darcy."

Anne kept pacing and thinking. The trouble was, vengeance required knowledge and she didn't know all that much about her cousin, despite his being a relation. Only a couple years older than her and Darcy, Richard had always been a part of their games, but his older brother Henry almost never was. He'd declared long ago that it was beneath his dignity both as a male and a future earl to play with a girl, no matter that Anne ran, fished, spit, and cursed just as well as any boy, and better than most. But Henry was always like that. Full of his own importance. That's why he thought he could get away with taking her apple tart.

"We need to know what's valuable to him," she muttered. "What does he care about the most?"

"Right now, he's very keen on the stablemaster's daughter," Richard said. He dipped down and plucked up two fresh pieces of grass.

"Our stablemaster's?" Anne asked.

"Yes. He says she's blossomed into a woman since the last time we visited here."

Anne pulled a face at that. "What a terrible thing to say, and to have happen to you." She shuddered. "I certainly hope I don't do any blossoming."

Darcy let out a laugh. "I hardly think that will happen. I mean, look at you."

Anne paused in her pacing to look down, taking in

her boots and riding habit. A wide belt clasped her scrawny waist, from which her hunting knife and a bag of powder hung. Her nails were chipped and not entirely clean, and she doubted her face was either. Her thick hair hung in a single braid and she wore a cap, rather than a bonnet, as bonnets were rubbish for playing games with her cousins.

"I look perfectly well," she snapped and resumed pacing. "So, we know Henry fancies the stablemaster's daughter. Does she fancy him?"

"She must," Darcy said, picking at a piece of bark. "He's going to be an earl."

Anne nodded. "That's true." She'd seen plenty of women try to attract her papa in the years since her mother's death. As most of them didn't know him at all, she could only conclude that what they liked about him were things other than him, so the same would go for her older cousin.

Richard blew into his new concoction, two shrill whistles sounding at once. Dropping his hands, he grinned. "It worked. I wonder if I can do three."

Anne halted her pacing. "We don't need her to fancy him."

"We don't?" Darcy asked.

"Not for my plan to work." A grin split her face.

"Why do I think this is going to end with us in trouble?" Darcy muttered.

Richard paused in his hunt around the base of the elm for three perfectly matched blades of grass. "Because Anne's plans always do," he said and resumed searching.

"We will need some fine rope, a gown and bonnet such as the stablemaster's daughter would wear, all the ink in the house, a bucket, a lot of straw, and for one of you to tell Henry that the stablemaster's daughter wants to meet him tonight."

"Does she want him to?" Darcy asked.

Anne shrugged. "How should I know? Let's hope not, because it will ruin my plan if she's there."

Darcy frowned down at her. "I'm not going to lie to Henry."

"Well I can't tell him," Anne protested. "He won't believe me, if he even listens. He never listens to a thing I say. He probably didn't even hear me say that we each got two of the apple tarts." Although he must have, or why smirk at her as he shoved her tart into his mouth?

"I'll do it," Richard said, plucking a blade of grass.

"You're going to lie to your brother?" Darcy's tone held condemnation.

Richard shrugged. "He lies to me all the time, and to Father."

"But he's going to be an earl someday," Darcy protested.

"What has that to do with anything?" Anne demanded. "Richard said he will do it, and that's all that matters to my plan. Now come down here, Darcy. You're the most careful, so you must find a bucket and go around the house and collect all the ink. We need the bucket as full as possible. I'll get the gown and bonnet from the wash, because I'll be noticed the least there, and you can get the rope, Richard. We'll meet outside the stables tonight. And Richard, whatever you say to Henry, see that it gets him there at eleven."

Darcy frowned down from his perch. "What if someone is in the stables? Won't they want to know why we're there?"

Anne shrugged. Only the night groom would be

there, and he was always asleep. "If anyone asks, tell them we're making a scarecrow."

"Are we making a scarecrow?" Darcy asked, swinging down from the tree.

Anne exchanged a look with Richard, silent commiseration over the inconvenience of Darcy's scrupulous honesty, then nodded. "Yes. We're making a scarecrow, Darcy."

CHAPTER TWO

Pilfered gown and bonnet bundled under her arm, Anne peered as far into the night as the ring of light cast by her lantern permitted, waiting for Richard and Darcy. Finally, they came down the hill to the stable, their own lantern bobbing. Richard held the light aloft, a skein of rope slung over his shoulder. Darcy carried a bucket before him with both hands. He walked with exaggerated care, obviously worried about spilling the contents. Anne hoped that meant he had a lot of ink.

"How long will this take?" Darcy asked as they approached. "We're meant to have retired for the evening."

"Less time if you don't squander it asking questions." Anne pulled out a pocket watch, checking the time. It was a quarter past. "Richard, will Henry be here at eleven?"

He nodded. "He should be, but he's always late."

Satisfied, Anne turned to march into the stable, empty except for the lone groom who snored in the tack room, there in case anything startled the horses. Or on the off chance that Anne's father urgently required a saddled mount at an odd hour, which hadn't happened since her mother died, a night faded in the mists of a three-year-old's memory.

She went in, passing between stalls that held mildly curious horses. When she neared the back, she set her lantern and the gown and bonnet on the floor, then started up the ladder to the hayloft. Looking over her shoulder, she called softly, "I'll throw down some hay. We have to gather it up to stuff the gown and bonnet."

Anne started on the hay, Richard and Darcy working together to stuff the gown. They had to tie it closed weirdly in several spots, so Anne left the hayloft and sneaked into the tack room. She added the sleeping groom's boots, which he'd removed before bedding down on a pile of tack, an old pair of gloves, and a horse blanket to their so-called scarecrow. By the time they were finished, with about fifteen minutes to spare, their straw lady looked as though she would do.

"Now what?" Richard asked, dusting chaff from his trousers.

"Now we stand her down here with a lantern behind her." Anne picked hers up and moved it deeper into the stable, while Richard and Darcy brought their creation. "This way, she'll be a silhouette. He won't be able to tell she's not real until he reaches her." After a moment's hesitation, she shuttered the lantern more, so only a little light got out.

"So, he'll be embarrassed that he came to meet a stuffed woman?" Darcy nodded. "Fair enough, but I bet you that if George were here, he would have come up with a better plan."

Anne snorted. Darcy's friend at Pemberley, George Wickham, could never out-imagine her. Even at fourteen, he only thought about skirts and coin, and while he could invent fun games, when they played them somehow everyone always got into trouble except him. Not taking the punishment for your idea was cowardly. "Hardly. And anyhow, that's not the plan. A little private embarrassment is nowhere near the revenge I seek. Richard, give me the rope. Darcy, get the bucket and take it up into the hayloft."

Calling on the lessons of her father's huntsmen and working as quickly as she could, Anne strung the rope across as a tripwire, going all the way up to the bucket. This, she walked out onto a beam to place, ignoring Darcy's warnings that she would fall, as if walking on a squared off beam weren't easier than traversing the limbs of a tree. If all went according to plan, Henry would be drenched in ink and stained for days. Anne's face split into a wide grin as she walked carefully back along the beam to the loft, where Darcy and Richard waited with the second lantern.

She jumped down to the safety of the loft floor and pulled out her watch, then angled it to catch the light. "He'll be here any moment. Quick, let's hide in the hay and close the lantern."

"I only just got all the chaff off me," Darcy grumbled but wiggled down into the hay between her and Richard.

Richard closed their lantern, plunging the loft into darkness. Now, only the glow from Anne's lantern, placed far down the aisle on the other side of the straw lady, illuminated the stable. Anne peered down, feeling that their fake stablemaster's daughter looked quite real, insofar as silhouettes went.

Straw poked through her riding habit, making her itch. Darcy pulled out a handkerchief and blew his nose. Anne cast him a fierce look he probably couldn't see in the darkness. He was not going to ruin this for her because hay made his nose itch.

"How long do—" Darcy began.

Anne elbowed him in the ribs, hissing, "Shh."

From somewhere without came the sound of whistling. Anne held her breath as the sound neared, certain it was Henry. A tall figure strolled in, a bottle of wine in one hand and two of her father's crystal glasses in the other.

Henry halted, the whistling stopping as well. "Is that you, my dear?" he called.

The straw woman did not reply.

Below, Henry peered into the near darkness. "Don't play coy with me. I got your message."

With all her heart, Anne willed him forward.

Finally, with a shrug, Henry set off down the aisle between the rows of stalls. Sleepy-eyed horses watched him pass.

He hit the tripwire and stumbled. Arms wheeling, he dropped to his knees, the wine bottle landing with a loud clunk and the two glasses shattering. The bucket toppled. Ink streamed down.

Right onto Henry's head.

Anne shoved her hands against her mouth, trying to hold in her laughter.

Henry let out a loud yell, and a curse, causing several of the horses to huff and stamp in their stalls. He brought up a hand to wipe at his face, then stared at his now-blue palm. A string of invectives left him.

He shoved to his feet. "Where are you, de Bourgh? I swear, I'll tan your hide, you cursed hoyden."

"You'd have to catch me first, Henry, and you've eaten too many tarts. You're too slow," Anne called, no longer able to be silent.

Richard snickered.

"That was spectacular," Darcy whispered. "He'll be stained blue for a week. We're going to be in so much trouble."

"You're in so much trouble," Henry roared, unknowingly echoing Darcy's words. He pushed a hand through his hair, flicking ink everywhere.

"Oy, what's going on in here?" the groom's voice called. He stepped from the tack room in his stockinged feet, a lantern held high. "Lord Henry, is that you?"

"Of course it's me, you dimwit."

"What happened, my lord?"

"Your master's chit of a daughter set a trap for me, obviously." He raised his voice to call, "And if I find out either of you are up there with her, Richard, Darcy, I'll see you get hell, too. This is not funny. Is this ink? My coat is ruined. My shirt and trousers as well, and there is glass all over the stable floor."

"It's not my fault you stole glasses out of my father's house to use in your seduction of an innocent girl," Anne called.

"Hardly innocent, if she invited me to the stable," Henry sallied back, then turned to look at the still motionless straw woman. He let out another curse. "She isn't real."

Anne dissolved into laughter. He'd only now realized that?

"We'll see what our fathers have to say about this, de Bourgh," Henry snapped. He pivoted and thudded his way out of the stable, dripping ink as he went.

"I can't believe that worked," Richard said, laughing. "Did you see his face? I've never seen him that angry."

"Or that shade of blue," Darcy said dryly.

Anne dissolved into laughter.

"Hey, who's up there?" the groom called, raising his

lantern. "You lot come down here right now and start cleaning up this mess. I'd best follow Lord Henry. Heaven preserve us if he walks through the house like that, ruining carpet and who knows what all as he goes."

Some of Anne's laughter left her at that. She hoped Henry would be smart enough not to go into Rosings dripping ink. Then she truly would be in trouble. With a sigh, she sat up. "I'll go down and start sweeping. You two sneak back to your rooms. No sense in all of us catching it."

"Nonsense." Darcy sat up too, a dark form in a barn once again lit only by Anne's nearly shuttered lantern below. "We helped. We will not shirk punishment while you shoulder all the blame."

"Besides," Richard said. "It was worth it." He unshuttered the lantern.

Anne took in the laughter in Richard's eyes and the determination on Darcy's face and shrugged. "Don't say I didn't try to let you get out of this." She stood and went to shimmy down the ladder. Clean-up was going to take a while.

CHAPTER THREE

Anne stood on the carpet before her father's desk, Darcy and Richard alongside her. They were into the wee hours of the morning, and she had to stifle a yawn as her father's lecture continued. Sir Lewis, in a robe and nightclothes, didn't sit at his desk. Rather, he stood before it, flanked by Uncle Matlock and Uncle George. All three appeared quite grim, though Anne liked to think her father only pretended.

The only person in the room who was seated, Henry, glowered from the corner of one of the large leather couches. Fortunately, he had not tracked ink all over Rosings. He had been cleaned, though. His blue-stained hair gleamed wet from his scrubbing, and he wore fresh clothes. Anne wondered if that was a good idea or if being on him would turn his shirt blue.

And blue he was, even after bathing and changing his clothes. A great swath of color covered a third of his face, with a myriad of drips tracking like tears down his forehead and cheeks. Anne thought he looked quite wonderfully chastened by her vengeance, even if he did glower at her.

"So, you're telling me this is all because of a berry tart?" Her father said as the strident tones of his lecture waned. He waved a hand in Henry's direction. "You do realize that you could simply have asked for more to be made?"

"It's the principle of the thing, Papa," Anne said.

"We'd agreed that we each got two, but he ate his very fast and then took mine. And they were apple."

Sir Lewis scowled and scrubbed his hands over his face.

"They must be punished," Henry said in a sullen voice.

"Aye," Uncle Matlock said. "Do you have any idea of the cost of your little venture? The amount of ink soaked into the stable floor? The garb you stole for your straw figure can be salvaged, but Henry's clothing is ruined."

"Unless he wants a purple shirt and cravat," Richard said.

"This isn't amusing, Richard," Uncle Matlock snapped. "Your brother's face is going to be blue for days. This whole escapade rather leads me to believe that the clergy won't be for you. No, my lad, you'll be off to the regulars the moment you turn eighteen."

Richard looked down at the carpet, but Anne imagined him to be secretly pleased. He'd complained to her and Darcy often enough that he wanted to be a soldier, not a man of the cloth. Maybe, just maybe, she'd actually helped him.

"And you, Fitzwilliam." Uncle George let out a long, disappointed sigh. "I've raised you better than this."

Darcy nodded, his expression miserable. He, too, dropped his gaze to the floor.

Anne's father frowned at her. "You, miss, are not getting another berry tart, or apple, or any such confection until I feel you've learned your lesson."

"That's all?" Henry cried from his couch. "You can bet the whole thing was her idea. You should take a switch to her."

Sir Lewis turned a frown on him. "I am not beating

my daughter. Her mother believed that young women should be raised to have strong wills and I will honor my Catherine's wishes."

Uncle George snorted. "Strong, certainly, but we'll never get Darcy to marry her if she keeps on like this. You're ruining the girl. And she is a girl, Lewis. You seem to forget that."

Anne's father frowned. "Nonsense. If Darcy grows into a real man, he'll want a wife who can challenge him, not kowtow to his whims."

Anne watched her uncles exchange a look at that, and imagined they took offense at the statement, as her mother had been the only one of the three wives to ever gainsay her husband. Anne's namesake, her aunt Lady Anne Darcy, had been a quiet, sweet-natured woman. The Countess of Matlock wouldn't have been able to decide between white and red without looking to her husband, let alone muster an opinion on anything about which one might argue.

"Regardless," the earl said firmly, "George and I believe the girl needs a companion. Some influence of the female persuasion. In fact, we insist."

Sir Lewis bristled. "You insist?"

Uncle George nodded. "I'm afraid we do. Hire her a governess. Or a companion. Anyone, really, so long as she has excellent references and wears a skirt."

Anne's father drew in a great huffing breath, as if he would yell. He looked at her, then at Henry with his blue face, and let his breath back out slowly. "Very well. I will hire a companion for Anne."

Dread lodged in Anne's gut. She had no idea what having a companion entailed, but if it had anything to do with making her act like other young ladies, or blossoming, it was going to be absolutely dreadful.

"Excellent," the earl said. "All that's left is for apologies to be issued. Richard, apologize to your brother."

Richard stepped forward and turned to Henry. "I'm sorry about your coat and shirt and trousers, and your face. I see now that what we did was wrong and offer my sincerest apologies."

Henry nodded, his face still twisted in anger. He slanted a look at the three men who presided over their little court and muttered, "Apology accepted."

"Fitzwilliam," Darcy's father said, gesturing to Henry.

Darcy stepped up and turned to stand shoulder to shoulder with Richard. "I, too, am sorry. I'm ashamed of my actions, and doubly beg forgiveness for not considering the expense and inconvenience of taking all the ink in the house. I apologize to you, Henry, and to you, Uncle Lewis. You can be assured that nothing of this nature will take place again."

Anne rolled her eyes ceilingward.

"That's alright, Darcy," Henry said, sounding more sincere than he had when addressing Richard. "I know none of it was your idea."

"I still should not have gone along with it," Darcy said firmly.

"Yes, well, all is forgiven, lad," Anne's father said. He turned to her. "Anne?"

"Yes, Papa?"

"It is your turn to apologize to Henry."

"No."

Her father's brow creased. "What do you mean, no?"

"He wronged me, and he deserved what he got, and I am not sorry."

"That is not an acceptable answer, miss," her father barked. "Apologize this instant."

"Only after he apologizes to me for taking my apple tart." Taking in her cousin's blue face, Anne did feel as if she'd perhaps punished him more severely than he deserved, and she understood that she'd ruined his clothing as well and wasted a lot of ink, which was precious even in a wealthy household, not to mention the crystal glasses.

But she refused to relent. Henry had wronged her, and all she'd done was take vengeance.

"Very well, then." Her father straightened to his full height.

Anne's eyes went wide. Would he actually beat her?

"Tomorrow morning, I am summoning a companion for you. You will learn to be a lady when required. Furthermore," he pointed at her, a dire gesture if ever Anne had seen one. "No hunting, fishing, or shooting of any kind for a month."

Her jaw hinged open. "But Papa."

Sir Lewis's eyes were hard. "Don't 'but papa' me, miss. You've brought this upon yourself."

"But Richard, Darcy, and I are to go hunting tomorrow. They'll only be visiting a fortnight more and this will be our first proper hunt."

"I don't care if this is their last visit to Rosings ever. You are not hunting with them."

"It's my last visit," Henry muttered.

Not seeming to have heard, Sir Lewis continued. "Nor will it matter how long they are to remain, because I daresay my man in London can have a suitable companion here in three days, and once she arrives, you'll be far too busy learning to behave to have time to hunt. What say you to that?"

Anne pursed her lips, anger boiling up in her. "You mean to say that this companion will arrive regardless, and that my only chance to hunt with Richard and Darcy before she does is to apologize to Henry?"

"Precisely." Sir Lewis glared down at her, his expression set.

To either side of her father, Anne's uncles also stood tall, both appearing pleased and perhaps even impressed.

She drew in a long, slow breath. Turning, she marched past her co-conspirators, then whirled to face them. Her back to Henry she said, "Richard, Darcy. I regret to inform you that I will be unable to hunt with you for the remainder of your visit here. I apologize for this short notice to the change in my plans. Hopefully, it will not be too inconvenient for you." Chin high, Anne marched from the room.

CHAPTER FOUR

Mrs. Jenkinson was tall, too thin, and worn-looking, as if someone had taken a normal height, middle-aged widow and stretched her to form the being before Anne. She wore mourning gray, although she couldn't have been widowed at all recently because Anne had seen her references on her father's desk, and though she hadn't been allowed to read them, they'd appeared extensive. As well they would be, for Sir Lewis wouldn't hire just anybody to be Anne's companion. Mrs. Jenkinson must be quite reputable.

Anne disliked her immediately.

"You should offer to send for tea and then we should be seated," Mrs. Jenkinson said after she and Anne had faced each other across the drawing room for several minutes.

"Should I?" Anne made the query simply to be contrary. She might not have a mama, but she was well aware that ladies sat around drinking tea. And chattering endlessly. It was going to be horrible.

"Yes." Mrs. Jenkinson regarded her without expression. "And then we will begin with comportment, which I daresay must itself begin with poise and how to pour. That is, unless you feel that pouring tea properly will be beyond your abilities at this stage?"

Anne pressed her lips together, then turned and marched over to yank on the bell pull. Deeper inside

Rosings, a chime sounded. In moments, a maid appeared.

"We would like tea, please," Anne said. The girl curtsied and left, so Anne returned her attention to her new nemesis, Mrs. Jenkinson. "Would you care to be seated?"

Mrs. Jenkinson glided forward with impressive smoothness for someone who knew neither how to fence, box, or, Anne suspected, even ride well. She came to a halt before a settee and waited.

Knowing what was expected of her, Anne moved to take a similar position on the opposite side of the low table set in the center of the room. What she didn't know, because no one had told her and she and her father called on others so rarely, and only invited those who were relations, was who was meant to sit first.

So she stood there, glaring across the table at Mrs. Jenkinson.

After a long moment, and with the slightest twitch of her mouth that might have been a suppressed smile, Mrs. Jenkinson sat.

Anne flopped down onto her settee.

"Head up. Shoulders back. Spine straight." Mrs. Jenkinson's eyebrows went up and she added, "Legs together and crossed at the ankles, please. You have fourteen years. You are a young lady. Sit like one."

Anne let out a long sigh and complied.

Mrs. Jenkinson said nothing about the sigh, although Anne had expected her to, and instead looked Anne up and down. "Normally, we would speak of the weather, but as ours is to be an extended acquaintance and of an instructional nature, let me begin with a question. I am told you like to fence?"

Anne sat straighter still, much happier to speak of fencing than of the weather. "I do." A sudden wariness filled her. Was this woman going to tell her she couldn't fence anymore? Would she be able to convince Anne's Papa of as much? Anne would not stand for that.

"In fencing, I understand poise, comportment, and form are paramount. Is that true?"

Anne nodded. "Most certainly. That's why I'm better than Henry. I maintain proper stances and engage in well-executed movements. He's strong, but sloppy."

"Well, tea is no different."

Anne pulled a face.

Mrs. Jenkinson didn't appear to notice, although she couldn't help but do so. "You must think of the parlor as a training ring," she said. "Each movement is staged, precise, and important. Your posture doubly so."

"But that's silly. No points are scored. No one wins at tea."

"That is unquestionably not true." Mrs. Jenkinson held up a hand when Anne would have protested. "Once you have received enough instruction to understand what you are witnessing, you and I will call on a neighbor. We will begin with the parson and his wife. I hear their daughter, her husband, and their three grown daughters are visiting. They will be a suitable first foray. You will learn, Miss de Bourgh, that tea is as much a stratagem as a fencing bout or a game of chess."

Anne figured her new companion exaggerated but at least Mrs. Jenkinson made tea seem a little bit interesting. Still, to call on the old parson and his wife?

"I suppose I can learn a bit about pouring tea, but must we go to Hunsford? Mr. Galloway is so old, and it smells like soup there."

"I deem the parsonage the perfect place for your first foray into behaving properly at tea. Especially with the contingent from London visiting. With any luck, the girls will be the very image of surety, and will be harsh in their judgment of others. That will give you a taste of what you might expect from a London Season."

"I'm not ever having a Season." Maybe if Anne set Mrs. Jenkinson straight on that, she would give up on these tea pouring lessons. "Eventually I'll marry Darcy. Our fathers have agreed on it. Uncle Matlock says so, too. The three of them decided it years ago."

"That does not mean you won't have a Season."

Outside, horns rang out, followed by the baying of the hounds. Anne sighed. Darcy and Richard would be hunting. They were free to ride and shoot. To climb trees and sit by the pond, skipping stones or fishing. And here she was, stuck inside talking about Seasons and marriage and tea.

This was the worst day ever.

She leveled a glare on Mrs. Jenkinson. "I won't have a Season."

"We shall see. I find it's best to be prepared for all eventualities."

The maids came in then, setting out the tea things, and Mrs. Jenkinson's talk turned to how to brew the tea and which imaginary guest should be served first. Things Anne had never bothered to think about, because who would want to, were apparently the keys to life itself. Silly nonsense such as if Anne should hold her saucer or only lift her teacup. If dishes should be passed to the left or right. If her teaspoon should move up or down or from side to side or in a circle, as if the sugar cared which way she stirred it.

Somewhere in the distance shots rang out and the hounds bayed. Anne felt certain the hunt went well. Being stuck inside with Mrs. Jenkinson and her comportment lesson was almost enough to make Anne wish she'd apologized to Henry. Almost.

And it was definitely enough to make her realize she had to get rid of Mrs. Jenkinson. How, she didn't yet know, but Anne would figure it out. If tea was a game of chess, Anne would play it, and learn about her adversary, and concoct something so horrible, Mrs. Jenkinson would be fleeing by the end of the week. That would give Anne a whole sennight to go back to having fun with her cousins.

CHAPTER FIVE

Several nights later when the clocks struck two, Anne was at her bedroom window, lantern in hand. She unshuttered the lantern once. Twice. Then a third time. That was the signal. She waited, peering out, down the side of Rosings. From a room at the far end a light shone and went out. Then again, and again. The same sequence was repeated from another room, a few windows down. Grinning, Anne picked up her lantern, opened the shutter just enough to be able to see, and slipped from her bedchamber.

She went down to the library, not beating Darcy and Richard there, as the guest rooms and their staircase were at that end of the house. Both wore nightclothes and belted robes, as did Anne. All three were meant to be abed.

When she entered, Darcy stood from the couch on which he sat and bowed. "Anne."

Anne halted, scrunching her nose. "What's that about?"

"My father says I should treat you like other young ladies so that you will become one."

Anne rolled her eyes.

"Anne's never going to be a young lady," Richard said from where he lounged in an armchair. "Now come on, why did you call a meeting?"

"I think I've found a way to get rid of Mrs. Jenkinson," Anne said gleefully.

Darcy shook his head. "I am not dyeing your

companion blue."

Anne gave him a pitying look. "Don't be silly. Papa hasn't got enough ink in yet, and it would be pathetic to use the same prank twice. I would be ashamed of us."

"And I don't think Mrs. Jenkinson would be interested if I told her that the stablemaster's daughter asked me to pass along the details of a clandestine meeting," Richard added.

His expression offended, Darcy said, "I wasn't thinking we would ink her in the stable."

"It doesn't matter where we would ink her because we're not doing that." Anne moved to the table to set down her lantern so she could pace. She always thought better when she was moving. "On our way back from that dreadful tea at the parsonage, I learned that she's afraid of slugs."

"Slugs?" her cousins chorused.

Anne waggled her fingers in the air. "You know, great big slimy slugs."

"And we're going to...?" Darcy asked, trailing off.

"Catch a lot of slugs, for a start," Anne said, pacing before the table. "I've been talking to the gardener about how one does, you know. Apparently, they like ale."

"That makes sense," Richard said from his chair. "Henry likes ale."

Anne laughed. "That does make sense."

"And then we put them all in her bed?" Darcy asked, sounding uncertain.

Anne shook her head. "No. She'd only know it was me. We have to be more sneaky than that. I want to put one in her bed. And in a shoe. In her dress pocket. But not all at once. Maybe four slugs a day."

"She'll still be suspicious," Richard said. "Let's begin with just one, then wait a day and do two. Then three the next day, and then ten."

Anne paused in her pacing to grin at him. "That's a good plan. That will really upset her, always searching for where the next slug might appear."

Richard leaned forward in his chair. "And we should come up with a story. Something about slugs and witches."

Anne shook her head. "A story is a good idea, but she won't believe in witches. Maybe something about how slugs get in because the stonework is poor."

Richard frowned. "I like the idea of witches."

"This seems like something we'll get into trouble for," Darcy said.

"How?" Anne paced away, thinking about stonework and witches. "We aren't responsible for all the slugs in the world."

"But we will be," Darcy said.

"But no one will know," she countered.

"Anyhow, I don't see why you need our help." A glance showed Darcy looking mutinous, his arms crossed over his chest. "And collecting slugs will not help you to become more ladylike, Anne."

"Bother ladylike," Anne snapped. "I want to go hunting and fishing and climb trees, like we do every summer. I do not need lessons on how to pour tea. You like me fine, don't you? How I am? So why would I change."

Darcy shrugged. "Yes. I like you fine."

Anne kept pacing. "Then who cares how I pour tea."

Apparently, Darcy didn't have an answer to that because he gave none, but after a moment he reiterated, "But why do you need our help?"

Anne stuck up her thumb. "First, because I can't seem to get outside without her following me." She added another digit. "Second, because I can't always be there when she finds slugs, or disappear right before she finds them, or she'll know it's me and she won't be scared. Sometimes, I have to be with her, and they have to be left in wait, so she won't know where they came from." She added one more finger. "And third, because we need to steal some ale. It's all locked up at night and I can't get the key from the housekeeper, so we need to get it in the daytime and that means a distraction and a lookout."

"I call distraction," Richard said.

Anne nodded. Darcy made a much better lookout, as their usual distraction when pilfering from the kitchen was for Richard to chat with the kitchen maids. Darcy wasn't good at talking with girls even though, of late, Anne had noticed that they didn't seem to mind his awkwardness as much. She wondered if it would be like with her father. That women would want Darcy for things that weren't him. He wasn't to be an earl like Henry or a Sir like her papa, but he did live in a very nice house.

But she was to marry him, so she imagined he would be safe enough, and none of that mattered right now. Now was for planning and slugs.

"How about ghosts," Richard said. "I mean, if we can't have witches."

"I think ghosts are even less likely to have slugs," Darcy said.

Richard shrugged. "Well, it has to be something scary."

"We'll have plenty of time to talk about what story

to tell while we make the slug traps," Anne said. "Tomorrow we'll get the ale. Then we'll need some serving dishes. They can't be too deep, or the slugs will drown. Just deep enough to hold some ale. We have to put them out at night and collect the slugs really early in the morning, before the sun drives them off, and then we'll need a slug container. Something with dirt in it and a lid."

"My father has some hat boxes," Darcy said. "We could take the hats out and use those."

Anne smiled, happy he'd given up worrying about getting in trouble and joined in the planning. "Good. You get the hat boxes and you and Richard can put in some dirt. Where should we hide them?"

"We can put them in the back of the garden under that weeping beech," Richard said. "No one goes under there but us."

"And we can surprise her with a few at a time." Anne grinned again, going back over Richard's plan of how to introduce the slugs to make them the most scary. "This is going to be the best prank ever."

Richard grinned too. "Definitely."

Darcy sighed. "We're going to be in so much trouble."

CHAPTER SIX

"If you can best Lord Henry, and you can beat Master Fitzwilliam, why can you never win against Master Richard?" Mrs. Jenkinson asked as they walked the garden path.

Even though Mrs. Jenkinson spoke on one of Anne's favorite topics, she found it difficult to focus. They'd pilfered the ale and serving platters and had an excellent haul of slugs. Darcy had suggested, brilliantly, that the first one should appear out of doors to make it all more believable, so he and Richard said they would leave a really big one right in the middle of the path, and Anne and Mrs. Jenkinson were nearly there. The slug would be around the next bend.

"Well," Anne said, gathering her thoughts. She had to appear normal, or she would ruin everything. "I can beat Henry because he's sloppy, as I told you, and I can beat Darcy because he's too rigid. He tries to do the sequences too perfectly. Once he starts one, he won't stop, so if you switch in the middle, you have him. But Richard is very quick, and he has a good imagination. He'll think of something new to do that I haven't seen before and sometimes I can defend against it and sometimes I can't." A little annoyance shot through Anne as she added, "And he's a lot taller than I am. He has the reach on me."

"I would very much enjoy watching you practice, once your father lifts his injunction."

Anne sighed at that. After failing to force an apology from her by his hunting restriction, Sir Lewis had added fencing, boxing, and everything else Anne enjoyed. Except riding. Mrs. Jenkinson insisted healthy exertion benefited girls. Anne was grateful to her for that, and for her interest in fencing. Maybe she shouldn't . . . But no, she would have no real freedom until Mrs. Jenkinson was gone. The slug plan must move forward.

Focusing on their conversation, even as the curve in the path drew near, Anne said, "Well, it's more fun to watch when I can fence against Darcy or Richard than when it's only me and my fencing instructor. Especially Darcy. He makes this super intense, serious face, which is too funny not to—"

Mrs. Jenkinson screamed, jerking back and colliding with Anne. Her hands, vice-like, clamped around Anne's arm. Faintly, a snicker sounded. Fortunately, Mrs. Jenkinson didn't seem to hear as she stared down the path with a look of horror on her face.

Making her eyes round with innocence, Anne asked, "Mrs. Jenkinson, whatever is the matter?"

Prying a hand free, she pointed up the path.

There, right in the middle, was a big, fat, slimy slug. Anne fought against the need to grin. It was a beautiful specimen, all black and brown and striped and spotted.

Anne drew in a breath and spoke the words they'd agreed she would. "Oh dear. Are the slugs back?"

Mrs. Jenkinson squeaked out, "What do you mean, back?"

Anne shrugged. "A few years ago, we had the worst trouble with them. They filled the garden. Then they started turning up in the house. It was awful. Slugs everywhere."

"Everywhere?" Mrs. Jenkinson sounded faint.

Anne nodded, very serious. "Oh yes. Everywhere. I even found one in my chamber pot." That ought to scare her.

"I . . . may we go back the other way?" Mrs. Jenkinson took her other hand from Anne's arm and gestured at the house. "I can't walk past that thing."

"Yes. Certainly. And don't worry, I'll tell the gardener. I'm sure he'll know how to get rid of them, although the last one didn't. He left, actually, cursing slugs and saying he would never return." Rosings had the same gardener now as when Anne was born, but Mrs. Jenkinson didn't need to know that.

"Yes. Do tell him. Please ask him to keep them away from the house," Mrs. Jenkinson all but pleaded.

Gleeful, Anne solicitously looped her arm through her companion's and led her away.

After that, the real fun started. They did put a slug in her bed, and several in her slippers, not knowing which pair she would wear next. They put slugs in her bathing room, and in the pockets of her gowns. On her hairbrush, although Anne privately thought that one would crawl away before she found it, and once even on her plate during tea. Finally, as a coup de grâce, they engineered a stunt where Anne held Mrs. Jenkinson's bonnet for her while she put on her gloves when readying for a walk, thrust it behind her back where she stood in the parlor doorway, and Darcy and Richard filled it with slugs. Mrs. Jenkinson didn't glance inside. Simply put it on her head. Anne thought her screams would shatter the crystals in the entrance hall chandelier.

That may have been one step too far because Sir Lewis and Anne's uncles came running down the hall from the back parlor, where they'd been smoking and enjoying brandy after luncheon.

"What the devil is going on?" Sir Lewis roared. "Who is—" He broke off, taking in Mrs. Jenkinson's slug and tear covered face.

She lifted her chin, her mouth squeezed into a tight, disapproving line. "Sir Lewis, I am leaving at once. You will have to find someone else to tame this hoyden you have reared, for it will not be me. I have never been so abused in all my days."

"Oh dear," Uncle George murmured.

Uncle Matlock turned away, coughing, but his coughs sounded suspiciously like guffaws. Anne suspected that he alone of the gentlemen found the scene amusing.

"But, Mrs. Jenkinson," Sir Lewis began.

"No." She reached up, plucked a slug from her face, and held it out to the butler. "I am going now to pack." Grasping her skirt, she tramped up the stairs.

"Get a maid to assist Mrs. Jenkinson at once," Sir Lewis ordered the butler, who eyed the slug on his palm. "Anne, Richard, Fitzwilliam, to my study this instant."

"Darcy and Richard aren't here, Papa," Anne said staunchly.

"I don't believe that for a moment," Sir Lewis snapped. "And if they don't come out by the count of ten, I will label them the worst sort of cowards to let you take all the blame for this."

From each side of the parlor doorway, Darcy and Richard appeared. Anne pulled a face at them, certain her father had been bluffing. He couldn't have known for sure that they were there. She would have taken the blame.

"To my study," Sir Lewis reiterated, jabbing a finger in that direction.

Anne in the lead, they marched down the hall.

Once again, the three gentlemen arrayed before Anne's father's desk. Sir Lewis let out a long-suffering sigh. Rather than speak to her and her cousins, he addressed his peers. "Who knew raising children bereft of our wives would be so trying?"

"There is a solution," Uncle George said quietly.

Sir Lewis cocked an eyebrow. "Do tell."

"There is a school for girls, in Wales. They say it's quite strict. There's certainly no fencing or hunting." He eyed Anne. "There are only classes on comportment and hard-eyed school mistresses with rulers."

"I've heard of the place." Anne's father turned sad eyes on her, that emotion much scarier than the anger she'd expected. "In truth, I've looked into it before." Slowly, enunciating each word, he continued, "They don't even have a stable."

"No stable?" Anne swallowed, the gulping sound audible. "W-where do they keep the horses?"

"There are no horses," her father said in dire tones.

Anne's mouth hinged open.

Darcy stepped forward. "It was my fault. I came up with the idea. Anne hardly did a thing."

"Mine too," Richard added, joining him. He slanted a worried look at Anne. "That is, I helped Darcy. Anne really didn't even know what we were about."

"The two of you worked from Mrs. Jenkinson that she is afraid of slugs?" Matlock asked, his voice dire with disbelief. "Don't add lying to your list of transgressions, my boy."

Richard looked down, flushing.

"Yes, this school seems quite the thing," Anne's father said.

"Papa, you can't send me there. No fencing? No hunting at all? Not even riding? I'll die. I'll surely die."

"Save your dramatics, miss. My mind is made up. Bid your cousins farewell and go pack. The school is year-round, so I daresay you won't be seeing Richard and Fitzwilliam again anytime soon."

Anne met her father's implacable gaze for a long moment. His determination didn't waver. Dread settled in her gut. She truly had gone too far this time. She hung her head, more miserable than any time she could recall.

"I said, bid your cousins farewell, for you will take dinner tonight in your room and leave first thing tomorrow," her father stated. "I will send maids to help you pack. I daresay it won't take long. You won't need any riding habits or your fencing gear."

A lump lodged in Anne's throat. She swallowed it down, because she never cried. Not since she was little. She sucked in a long, deep breath, dashed at her eyes to ensure no tears brimmed there, and lifted her gaze. Her misery so acute as to be nauseating, she drew back her shoulders and turned to her cousins.

"Richard, Darcy. Apparently, it will be some time before I see you again." She halted, uncertain what more to say.

Darcy bowed to her. "Safe travels, Anne," he said quietly, looking nearly as miserable as she felt.

"Yes, safe travels." Richard bowed to her as well.

"Right then," Sir Lewis said. "Off you go. Straight to your room. No detours."

Her back rigid, Anne marched from the room. Behind her, she could hear her father saying, "Now, what will we do to punish the two of you?"

Anne went to her room and flung herself onto her bed, giving up on her resolve not to cry. She buried her face in her pillow, letting it soak up her sobs and her tears. When her maids came, she ignored them, though she could hear them packing. Finally, they left and she lifted her head, then went to her wash basin to bathe her face.

She couldn't believe her father was sending her away, and to such a horrible place. They'd only been slugs, and she knew for a fact that the maids always collected them and tossed them back out into the garden. No one had been harmed, even the stupid slimy slugs. Just, maybe, scared a little.

Anger filled her, mostly at Mrs. Jenkinson. Why did she have to scream like that? This was all her fault. Anne raged about her room, her anger filling the long, empty hours of the afternoon.

But by the time her dinner was brought, she was in a state of abject misery, angry at herself now. She shouldn't have been so mean to Mrs. Jenkinson. What had she been thinking, tormenting the woman with something she acutely feared? Her papa was right, Anne was terrible. A terrible monster who deserved to be sent away to Wales and never get to ride again, only pour tea.

More tears followed, and more misery. By the time her maid came to help her ready for bed, Anne acutely missed Mrs. Jenkinson. She hadn't been so bad, really. She'd only tried to help, and she'd defended Anne's right to ride, and had wanted to see her fence. Living with Mrs. Jenkinson at Rosings was incomparably better than going to some horrible school in Wales.

"Miss?" the maid queried, for Anne sat on her bed, her legs pulled up and a pillow clenched in her hands. "Should I brush out your hair?"

"No." Anne flung the pillow aside. "I am not going to bed yet. I must speak with my father. Where is he?"

"He and Lord Matlock and Mr. Darcy are in the green parlor, miss."

Anne nodded and jumped down from her bed. Her legs were half asleep from hours spent folded. She grabbed the bedpost for a moment to steady herself. The maid moved forward, hands out to help.

Anne brushed past her. She caught a glimpse in the mirror on her way by, the white-faced, disheveled girl there looking more like the ghost Richard had wanted them to make up than Anne. But she didn't care how she looked. She had to stop Mrs. Jenkinson from going away. She would promise to be good. Promise just about anything.

CHAPTER SEVEN

Anne marched through the manor house, fists balled at her sides and determination in her heart. She clattered down the great staircase and down the hall, passing several startled-looking servants along the way. The smell of cigar smoke coupled with knowledge to lead her to the back parlor where her father, Uncle Matlock and Uncle George waited.

She stomped in to find the windows open to permit fresh air, the floor-length curtains puffing inward in a light breeze. Ignoring her uncles, she stomped over to stand squarely before her father. He lowered his cigar and took a sip of brandy.

"Don't let Mrs. Jenkinson leave," Anne said.

Her father puffed at his cigar, his expression thoughtful. "I'm afraid she departed with alacrity."

Anne felt that as a blow to the gut, but she pressed on. "Then bring her back. I want her to teach me. Here, at Rosings."

"I'm afraid I already wrote to the school and promised a deposit."

"It cannot be that much. I will pay you back from my pin money."

"Hmm," her father drawled.

"What do you believe you could say to Mrs. Jenkinson to convince her to return?" Uncle George asked.

Anne whirled to face him, where he sat near one of the open windows. "I . . . I will apologize, to be certain.

And I will swear never to pull a prank on her again."

"And?" Uncle Matlock pressed when Anne faltered.

"And." Anne pursed her lips, thinking. "And I will swear to listen to her lessons and to do my best to learn them."

"Those are quite the promises," Sir Lewis said. "Why should I believe you can live up to them?"

Anne turned back to her papa. "Because I can. I swear, Papa. Please, bring her back. I'll be good. I promise, but don't send me away to Wales." To her shame, her voice cracked.

"You swear on your honor as a de Bourgh?" Sir Lewis's tone was very stern.

Standing straight and tall, Anne nodded. "I swear on my honor as a de Bourgh that I will behave regarding Mrs. Jenkinson, if only she will return and teach me, and I don't have to go to Wales."

"Very well, then," a feminine voice said.

Anne whirled to see Mrs. Jenkinson step from behind one of the curtains and could only gape at her.

"I accept your word, Miss de Bourgh," Mrs. Jenkinson said.

"You didn't leave," Anne gasped.

"Indeed, I did not." Leveling a stern look on Anne's father, she continued, "Sir Lewis may have fibbed."

"All in a good cause," Sir Lewis replied and stuck his cigar back in his mouth.

"But you were so upset and you said you would go," Anne pressed, thoroughly confused.

"This might help explain things." Mrs. Jenkinson pulled a folded page from her pocket and held it out. "It's one of my references."

Anne took the page and unfolded it, reading. "The Conservatoire de Paris?" Anne blinked several times.

"Isn't that a music school?"

"It is, but what I taught there was the art of the dramatic." Mrs. Jenkinson's mouth twitched. "Acting."

"You were . . . acting?" Anne's head spun. She whirled to look at her father.

He shrugged. "Don't glare at me, miss. It was Mrs. Jenkinson's idea. After meeting you, she came to me and declared that you would never learn until you were taught that you need to."

Indignation filled Anne. She turned back to thrust the page at Mrs. Jenkinson. "Are you even afraid of slugs?"

"I am not."

Uncle Matlock chortled. "Thought I'd given it away, earlier, when I mentioned Mrs. Jenkinson's fear of slugs. The look you gave me, Darcy," he added to Anne's other uncle.

"Well, none of our offspring are fools. After contemplation, I rather thought they would realize they hadn't mentioned the fear."

Uncle Matlock shrugged, still appearing amused.

"You planned this?" Anne pressed. "All of you? Together?" A terrible thought came to her. "Richard and Darcy, too?"

Mrs. Jenkinson shook her head. "No. They never had, and still have, no knowledge of our plan."

Anne looked about the room, astounded. "I can't believe it."

Her father smiled around his cigar. "And yet it's true. Don't think your uncles and I didn't play pranks in our day, miss."

"So I don't have to go to Wales?"

"I don't know if there even is such a school in Wales," her father admitted.

Relief made Anne's head spin. "And I can hunt and ride and fence with Richard and Darcy?"

"Now as to that," Uncle George said in stern tones, "We agreed not. You three were still in the wrong, even if we baited you into it. You certainly did not have to seize on Mrs. Jenkinson's pretend fear of slugs as a means to torment her, nor fill her bonnet with them, and your cousins definitely did not have to help."

Wide-eyed, Anne asked, "So, how will you punish us?"

"If I may?" Mrs. Jenkinson said.

All three men, and Anne, turned to her.

"I believe a fitting punishment would be lessons," Mrs. Jenkinson continued. "Not only for Miss de Bourgh, but for all three. Comportment. Dancing. All manner of endeavors in proper etiquette come to mind, many of them easier to teach to three than one, for they hinge on maneuvering through society."

Anne groaned.

"You gave your word, miss," Sir Lewis stated.

"I know, Papa." She heaved a sigh.

"Lesson one, ladies do not sigh in public," Mrs. Jenkinson said firmly, but amusement lurked in her gaze. She looked from gentleman to gentleman. "Leave the three in my hands, though the young men obviously only for the duration of your visits."

Sir Lewis shrugged, turning to Anne's uncles. Both nodded.

"I have no issue with the idea," Uncle George said.

"Nor I," Uncle Matlock seconded.

Mrs. Jenkinson executed what Anne imagined was a perfect curtsy. "Thank you, gentlemen." She turned to Anne. "Come, Miss de Bourgh. Let us see what we can do to put right your face and hair before bed."

"But no one's going to see me," Anne protested.

"A lady always looks her best." Mrs. Jenkinson put a hand on her back, half pushing her from the room.

Anne craned her neck to see over her shoulder, ruefully taking in the smug expressions of the three men. Grudgingly, she supposed she'd gotten what she deserved. "Darcy and Richard are not going to be happy with me," she muttered as she and Mrs. Jenkinson walked down the hall.

"I daresay they'll feel better about their lessons when they learn that part of each day will be spent out of doors and that there will still be riding, at least, and fencing."

"There will?" Anne asked, joy shooting through her.

"Young people need exercise," Mrs. Jenkinson said firmly.

Anne stepped lighter after that. The more she thought about it, the less terrible Mrs. Jenkinson's presence in her life seemed. Glancing at her companion as they neared the great staircase at the front of the house, Anne smiled. Mrs. Jenkinson wouldn't be so bad, and Anne truly did want to learn how tea in a parlor was as much of a game of strategy as chess or fencing. Richard and Darcy ought to learn, too. After all, they also didn't have mamas to teach them.

Nodding to herself as she went up the stairs, Anne decided she was happy Mrs. Jenkinson was there after all.

This adventure of Miss Anne de Bourgh's is a *Pride & Prejudice* variation prequel to *Mr. Darcy's Bookshop*, a Darcy and Elizabeth centered love story. I hope you enjoyed reading!

For a sneak peek of *Mr. Darcy's Bookshop*, read on…

Mr. Darcy's Bookshop

by

Summer Hanford

CHAPTER ONE

November, 1811

Fitzwilliam Darcy pushed his spectacles up on his nose, for they were forever slipping. A more finely crafted pair might better remain in place, but could he afford those, he would need none, for he would be back in Pemberley with more activities at hand than going over his shop records by tallow light. At Pemberley, he would read during the day, for pleasure, with bright sunlight streaming into finely furnished rooms. And if he wrote, there would be no need for cramped letters he could hardly make out, simply to save on watery ink and coarse paper.

Finishing with his records for the day, he snuffed out all the tallow candles but one, then carefully trimmed down the wicks. Rising from the counter at the front of the bookshop, he took the remaining candle and made a check of the doors, front and back, though why anyone would want to rob a bookseller he didn't know. Satisfied his wares were safe for the night, he took the cashbox and went up the back stairs to the room above, where he finished the watered ale and half-eaten hand pie he'd procured earlier that day.

Going to the other side of the room, he readied for bed, then blew out the candle. By memory and feel, he crossed back to his narrow cot and climbed beneath thin sheets. So far, November had been mild, but soon enough London would grow cold and cloaked in a smoky miasma, and Darcy would shiver in his sleep. Perhaps if he went to his cousin Richard...but no. He wouldn't put Richard in the position of being at odds with the patriarchs.

Darcy sought rest, his mind on books and ledgers and the price of tallow. It did not help that he had sold only a single volume today, most of which had been spent dusting to keep the shop in good order and to give him something to do. Nor was tomorrow likely to be much different, although soon patrons would trickle in, seeking gifts to take back to their country estates for the Yuletide. December would be a better month. It always had been in years past.

He listened to the light patter of rain on the eaves, well aware he would face the same worries on the morrow. And the next day, and the following. Every day would be thus, until he relented to his father's and uncles' command that he marry his cousin Anne de Bourgh. Though he certainly wished no harm to his kin, no matter how they tormented, sometimes Darcy liked to imagine how his circumstances would differ had his father, Matlock, and Sir Lewis had died when he was young, rather than his mother and his aunts. Surely, as a mother, Lady Catherine would have laid to rest this nonsense about Darcy and Anne marrying. Were she alive still, Anne would be happily wedded already, and Darcy would be free from his imagined obligation to espouse her. He was certain of it.

Darcy drifted off during his wistful musings, to wake cold and stiff shortly before dawn. He dressed for the day then stoked his small stove to heat water for tea, which he brewed in a chipped pot. The precious leaves and the heat to boil water for them were the one luxury he wouldn't do without, his morning cup far more important than a second blanket.

Later, down in the shop, he unlocked the front door and put out the sign, then returned to his dusting. He began with the low, chest-height shelving at the front of the shop, then moved on to the taller shelves in the back of the store. Dust and disorderliness, he'd found, were the greatest enemies of a bookshop, aside from a lack of patrons. Immersed in his work, he didn't consider that it was the third Monday of the month until much later when the front door opened, the bell jangling, to admit George Wickham.

Darcy started to scowl, then mastered the expression as a second man entered on Wickham's heels. An amiable looking fellow in his early twenties, with neither great height nor over-fine looks to distinguish him, but a cheerful air of affability. By his garb and his presence with Wickham, Darcy assumed him to be wealthy. Wickham had no use for companions he couldn't count on to foot the bills, no matter how much money Darcy's father showered him with.

"Darcy," Wickham greeted with false warmth, sauntering over to the short ladder on which Darcy stood to reach the highest shelves. "Hard at work, I see. Come down here and I'll introduce you."

Leaving the feather duster on the shelf, Darcy climbed down the ladder. He pulled out a handkerchief to wipe his hands.

"Bingley, may I present an old friend of mine, Fitzwilliam Darcy?" Wickham turned back to Darcy. "And this is Mr. Charles Bingley."

"Pleased to make your acquaintance," Mr. Bingley

said affably. "Darcy? Isn't that the name of your patron, Wickham? Any relation? I hear the Darcys are quite the thing in Derbyshire."

"Why yes, Fitz here is somewhat related to the Darcys in Derbyshire," Wickham said. He eyed Darcy sardonically and added, "He's a poor relation, though, to be certain. I come by once a month to check on him."

"Too good of you," Mr. Bingley said, looking about. "Fine shop you have here, Darcy."

"Thank you."

"Quite a lot of books, isn't it?" Mr. Bingley continued. "I wish my collection were larger, but I am an idle fellow, and though I have not many, I have more than I ever look into. Still, can't hurt to browse."

"You do that," Wickham said. "Darcy and I are due a chat."

"Books on horseflesh and fencing are up front on those back two shelves there," Darcy added, pointing to the front corner of the shop.

"Excellent," Mr. Bingley said and wandered in that direction.

Darcy turned to Wickham. "My father won't approve of you bringing me a customer."

"Bingley?" Wickham raised his eyebrows. "You heard him. He's not the reading sort. He's having a devil of a time at university."

"Is that where you found him? Haven't you finished at university yet?"

Wickham shrugged. "I recently decided to give law a go. Had to start all over. Your father was more than happy to sell off that living he wanted me to fill and give me the funds to further my education."

Darcy eyed the loathsome being before him and

wondered how much money Wickham had swindled from George Darcy this time.

"Five thousand," Wickham said, following Darcy's thoughts, for they knew each other well, having been raised nearly as brothers. "The living didn't go for that much but my dear, dear godfather wanted to ensure I am comfortable while at my studies, so he augmented the sum." Wickham leaned near, lowering his voice to say, "By the time you give up this ridiculous show of independence, you'll be begging to marry your hoyden of a cousin just to refill Pemberley's coffers, the way your father spends money on me."

"Anne is not a hoyden." Not that anything about Anne was why Darcy would never relent to his father's demand that they wed. They simply did not suit, and being cut off from his family's money wouldn't persuade Darcy that they did. He would never give in to his father's tyranny.

"Of course she is," Wickham countered. "She rides and hunts and shoots. I've only ever seen her in boots and a habit, a crop in hand. Your uncle raised her to be the son his late wife didn't give him, which is why I sympathize with you not wanting to wed her, but you'll get Rosings, man. Stop this ridiculous charade and get the banns read."

"Must we do this every third Monday?" Darcy asked. "I have dusting to do."

Wickham shook his head. "Who would have thought, back at Eton, that the great Fitzwilliam Darcy of Pemberley would spend his days dusting piles of worthless books."

"I take exception to the notion that books are worthless."

"Do you?" Wickham shrugged again. "Never found

a single one I liked. Well, not here. You don't stock any of those bawdy ones with the pictures that they bring back from India."

"No," Darcy said coldly. "I do not. This is a respectable establishment."

"This? Only by dint of you being here. We're in Cheapside, after all. It's a stone's throw to the grand import warehouses."

"Did you say import warehouses?" Mr. Bingley said, striding over with three books in hand. "Fine places, those. Always trying to convince my sisters to get their fabrics and feathers and whatnots there. All the modistes do. Why pay for the markup, I say."

Darcy agreed. The great open-air market in the center of the warehouse district was where he made many of his purchases, including his tea.

Wickham chuckled. "My dear fellow, you pay for the markup so everyone will know that you can afford to." He shook his head, his charming countenance molded into amusement, with just a touch of condescension. "How about you treat me to lunch and I'll expound on the subject for you? You have a lot to learn if you wish to properly disentangle from your roots in trade."

Mr. Bingley pulled a face. "Don't I know it. My sisters are constantly on about the same thing."

"Well, if there's anyone who can educate you on how to best employ money to appear every inch the gentleman, it's me." Wickham cocked an eyebrow at Darcy. "Wouldn't you agree, Darcy?"

"Yes," Darcy said dryly. "On that, Mr. Wickham and I can very much agree."

"Splendid," Mr. Bingley said cheerfully. "I'll let you take me under your wing, then."

Darcy shook his head, pitying the affable young man. Who knew what terrible advice Wickham would give, all the while taking Mr. Bingley for every penny he could get. It would almost be worth marrying Anne simply to be able to influence George Darcy against Wickham and his copious spending.

Almost.

Mr. Bingley held up the books. "I'll get these, Darcy."

"Don't you want to know how much they'll run you?" Wickham asked before Darcy could speak. "You want to make certain he doesn't take advantage of you." He smirked at Darcy.

Mr. Bingley chuckled. "Can't see as a fine fellow with the Darcy name would swindle anyone. I'll take them regardless of the cost."

"Very well," Darcy said stiffly. No matter how many years he'd been at his bookselling business, nor how much he truly needed funds, it always dismayed him to accept payment. He'd rather gift the books to Mr. Bingley. As things stood, he gave the man a discount to make up, in some small way, for the money Wickham would separate him from.

After Mr. Bingley made his purchase the two said their goodbyes, Wickham trailing his new friend out. He paused at the door, letting it swing closed behind Mr. Bingley, and looked back to say, "I'll report to your father that you remain stubbornly opposed to bettering your circumstances, then, shall I?"

"Do what you like," Darcy replied. "You always do."

Wickham grinned. "Yes. I do, don't I?" With a parting smirk, he left.

Through the shop window, Darcy watched the two stride away. Both were fashionably dressed. Both appeared to be gentlemen. Not that Wickham ever would be, no matter how much he spent on his clothes. Darcy only hoped he didn't fleece his new friend too badly. Charles Bingley seemed like a good, if overly trusting, sort of fellow.

Shaking his head, Darcy climbed back up on the ladder and returned to dusting. At least Wickham's visit had put a bit of money in the till. Not enough to be worth Wickham's badgering, but enough to eat for a week which, added to what Darcy had, would see him into the new year. Perhaps with the influx that would come with the Christmas season, he'd be set until March, when he and his cousin Richard would take their annual pilgrimage to visit their Uncle Lewis at Rosings, to endure his list of their failings and Anne's endless badgering for them to hunt with her.

The visit was always a strain, but a welcome break from the bookshop and a nice augmentation to Darcy's diet. He would eat more meat in one week at Rosings than during the remainder of the year, most of it hunted and brought down by Anne. As an added boon, after a week with her and Sir Lewis, Darcy's resolve to defy his father would be bolstered and he would be longing for the quiet occupation of his bookshop.

That thought in mind, he cheerfully dusted. His thoughts turned to the happier topic of the upcoming Yuletide and the influx of purchases he always saw at the end of the year. Who knew what new delights the year's end might bring?

I hope you enjoyed this sneak peek of *Mr. Darcy's Bookshop*, and I think you can guess what delights December might bring (Elizabeth. . . it's Elizabeth!)

Try *Mr. Darcy's Bookshop* today!

ABOUT THE AUTHOR

Summer Hanford

Summer Hanford writes gripping Epic Fantasy (Summer H Hanford), swashbuckling Historical Romance (L Summer Hanford), and best-selling Pride and Prejudice retellings (Summer Hanford). She lives in the Finger Lakes Region of New York with her husband and compulsory, deliberately spoiled, cats. The newest addition to their household, an energetic setter-shepherd mix, is (still) not appreciated by the cats but is well-loved by the humans.

Get Your Thank You Gifts - Sign Up for My Mailing List Today!

Visit: **www.summerhanford.com/pride-and-prejudice-variations/**